Racism Issues

Edited by Christina Hughes

Series Editor: Cara Acred

Vol. 74

Independence Educ

First published by Independence

The Studio, High Green, Great Shelford

Cambridge CB22 5EG

England

© Independence 2013

Photocopy licence

The material in this book is protected by copyright. However, the purchaser is free to make

multiple copies of particular articles for instructional purposes for immediate use within the

purchasing institution. Making copies of the entire book is not permitted.

British Library Cataloguing in Publication Data

Racism issues. -- (Issues today ; 74)

1. Racism--Great Britain--Juvenile literature. 2. Race

discrimination--Great Britain--Juvenile literature.

3. Multiculturalism--Great Britain--Juvenile literature.

4. Great Britain--Race relations--Juvenile literature.

I. Series II. Acred, Cara editor of compilation.

305.8'00941-dc23

ISBN-13: 978 1 86168 651 0

Acknowledgements

The publisher is grateful for permission to reproduce the following material. While every care has been taken to trace and acknowledge copyright, the publisher tenders its apology for any accidental infringement or where copyright has proved untraceable. The publisher would be pleased to come to a suitable arrangement in any such case with the rightful owner.

Chapter One: What is Racism?

What is racism? © Young Scot 2013, *Show Racism the Red Card* © Show Racism the Red Card 2012, *The Equality Act, making equality real* © Crown Copyright 2013, *Are the people in Britain ethnically diverse?* © Mandy Barrow 2011, *All together now?* © Equality and Human Rights Commission 2013, *Challenging discrimination* © Chesterfield Law Centre 2013.

Chapter Two: Exploring Racism

Racism in the classroom © About Equal Opportunities 2000-2013, *Eight-year-olds are suspended for race abuse in Derbyshire schools* © Courtesy of the Derbyshire Telegraph 2012, *What if they'd said 'Jew'?* © Cara Acred/Independence Educational Publishers Ltd.,

Police racism: 293 cases, five dismissals © Channel 4 News 2012, *Confronting indirect racism* © About Equal Opportunities 2000-2013, *Online racism* © FindLawUK 2012, *Jail for student in Muamba Twitter race rant a perversion of justice* © 1997-2013 Index on Censorship, *Racism in football* © Crown Copyright 2012, *Record number of 'racist' attacks on English in Scotland* © Simon Johnson/The Daily Telegraph, *White people paid more and ethnic pay gap widening* © 2012 Institute for Social & Economic Research, *One in three Brits admit they are racist* © OnePoll 2012.

Illustrations: page 3 is by Angelo Madrid and pages 16 & 26 are by Simon Kneebone. All other illustrations, including the cover, are by Don Hatcher.

Images: page 1 © Jason Doiy Photography, pages 7 © bamlou, page 10 © Alex Mathers, page 21 © skippyjon.

Editorial by Christina Hughes and layout by Jackie Staines, on behalf of Independence Educational Publishers.

Printed in Great Britain by MWL Print Group Ltd.

Cara Acred

Cambridge

May 2013

Contents

About *ISSUES* today

ISSUES today is a series of resource books on contemporary social issues, designed for Key Stage 3 pupils and above. This series is also suitable for Scottish P7, S1 and S2 students.

Each volume contains information from a variety of sources, including government reports and statistics, newspaper and magazine articles, surveys and polls, academic research and literature from charities and lobby groups. The information has been tailored to an 11 to 14 age group; it has been rewritten and presented in a simple, straightforward and accessible format.

In addition, each **ISSUES** today title features handy tasks and assignments based on the information contained in the book, for use in class, for homework or as a revision aid.

ISSUES today can be used as a learning resource in a variety of Key Stage 3 subjects, including English, Science, History, Geography, PSHE, Citizenship, Sex and Relationships Education and Religious Education.

About this book

Racism Issues is Volume 74 in the **ISSUES** today series.

Globally, the UK is viewed as a place of diversity and tolerance. In a recent poll, however, one in three Brits admitted that they are racist. Even students as young as eight have been suspended for racial abuse. This book explores the concept of racism and goes on to debate the issues associated with discrimination: Can white people be the victims of racism? Do we overreact and label banter as racism? What is Islamophobia? These ideas, and many others, are discussed within.

Racism Issues offers a useful overview of the many issues involved in this topic. However, at the end of each article is a URL for the relevant organisation's website, which can be visited by pupils who want to carry out further research.

Because the information in this book is gathered from a number of different sources, pupils should think about the origin of the text and critically evaluate the information that is presented. Does the source have a particular bias or agenda? Are you being presented with facts or opinions? Do you agree with the writer?

At the end of each chapter there are two pages of activities relating to the articles and issues raised in that chapter. The 'Brainstorm' questions can be done as a group or individually after reading the articles. This should prompt some ideas and lead on to further activities. Some suggestions for such activities are given under the headings 'Oral', 'Moral dilemmas', 'Research', 'Written' and 'Design' that follow the 'Brainstorm' questions.

For more information about **ISSUES** today and its sister series, **ISSUES** (for pupils aged 14 to 18), please visit the Independence website.

www.independence.co.uk

What is racism?

We've all heard the word being used, but what exactly is racism? ChildLine has broken it down and taken a look at racism, where it comes from, and how it can affect you.

Racism is treating someone differently or unfairly simply because they belong to a different ethnic community.

People can also experience racial prejudice because of their religion or nationality. Racism takes many different forms, including:

- ➢ personal attacks of any kind, including violence.
- ➢ written or verbal threats or insults.
- ➢ damage to property, including graffiti.
- ➢ inappropriate language.

Why are people racist?

Racism comes from a belief that one ethnic community is superior to other communities. This can then lead to abusive or aggressive behaviour towards members of another community on the basis of such a belief. That is how the slave trade began many years ago.

Racists tend to feel threatened by anyone who is from a different race, religion, or culture. It comes from ignorance and fear brought on by stereotypes.

The thing is, we are not born racist. It's not in our genes. It comes from the views and beliefs that develop as we grow up. We can be influenced by friends, family, newspapers, and society in general. If a child or young person grows up within a racist family, or has friends who are racist, they may believe that racism is normal and acceptable. But it's not!

Prejudice of any kind is usually based on ignorance and fear; often people have opinions on things they know nothing about, including people, religions and cultures.

How racism affects you

If a young person, like yourself, experiences racism of any kind, they can feel lonely and sad. As with bullying, they may try to avoid situations where racist behaviour could occur, they might pretend to be ill, play truant from school, or be scared to leave their house.

Racial prejudice is serious stuff and something that we all want to avoid. Most people in Scotland believe they are not racist and say they would like to live in a country free from prejudice.

That is why there are many ongoing campaigns to stamp out racism wherever it rears its ugly head eg. sport – *Show Racism The Red Card* and *Kick Racism Out Of Football*; employment – *One Workplace Equal Rights*; all areas of life – *One Scotland*.

Did you know that racism is an offence?

Yes it is! If you want to get technical, it's an offence under Section 18 of the Public Order Act 1986 for any person to use 'threatening, abusive or insulting words or behaviour' with the intention of inciting or stirring up racial hatred or if, in the circumstances, this is likely to happen.

Meanwhile the Crime & Disorder Act 1999 makes racial harassment a serious criminal offence in Scotland. Not only that, but it is also an offence to display written material, such as posters, in the same manner.

The Equality Act 2010 also makes it illegal to discriminate on the grounds of race, including in employment and in the provision of goods and services.

Most recent figures reveal that there has been a 10% increase in racist incidents in the past year.

In 2011/12 there were 5,389 racist incidents, compared with 4,911 in 2010/11.

In 2011/12, 44% of victims of a racist attacks were of Asian race - i.e. Indian, Pakistani, Bangladeshi, Chinese, or other Asian.

23 January 2013

The above information is reprinted with kind permission from Young Scot.
© Young Scot 2013

www.youngscot.org

Show Racism the Red Card

Anti-Racism Educational Pack.

An introduction to racism

Can white people suffer from racism?

Yes! Absolutely anybody can suffer from racism. We all have a **skin colour**, **nationality** and **culture** and many of us have a **religion**. This leaves every single one of us vulnerable to racism. It is important to mention that racism usually happens to people in a minority group so, whilst racism can happen to anybody, it is more likely to happen to people from minority ethnic groups in Britain, for example a Gypsy or Traveller, a Muslim, a black person or a Polish person.

Is it racism if someone makes fun of your hair colour?

No. This is a really common myth that a lot of young people believe. Lots of people get picked on for their hair colour, especially people who have ginger or red hair, but this isn't classed as racism. Racism only covers treating people badly because of differences in skin colour, religion, nationality and culture. However, it is still wrong for a young person to be picked on because of their hair colour and they should be encouraged to report this to a person who they know and trust.

Is it okay to call someone a 'Paki?

No definitely not! 'Paki' is a racist word no matter how, when and why people say it, even if they are using it to describe a local shop or newsagent. The word 'Paki' has been used as a weapon to hurt people and to make them feel different, unwelcome and not valued; it is very painful to those who it is targeted towards. Sometimes people use 'Paki' as a nickname and have no intention of hurting or upsetting anybody. However, if they had experienced this word being shouted at them whilst someone attacked them or spat in their face, would they want to hear it being used? For many people this word stands for racism, hatred and conflict, so for these reasons it should never be used.

If I am describing someone should I say black or coloured?

The term 'coloured' reminds people of a time when things were extremely unequal in Britain between black and white people, for example when black people tried to rent accommodation in the 1950s and 60s, there were often signs up in windows stating 'No Dogs, No Irish, No Coloureds'. In addition the word 'coloured' is not very descriptive and implies that white people are not of colour or that white is 'normal' and everyone else can be grouped into one category 'coloured'. Sometimes people seem frightened to use the word black and think it might be rude or even racist so it is important to allay their fears and encourage the use of 'black' instead of coloured or dark or tanned. A lot of young people question why we use the word black when people are not actually black, which is a really good point. It is important to point out that we call people white when they're not actually white, but we keep things simple and use the 'umbrella' terms black and white.

Where does racism come from?

What is an Asylum Seeker?

An Asylum Seeker is someone who has been forced to leave their country of residence because their life is in danger, perhaps because of political or religious reasons or because of war. If they come to the UK, they will have lodged an asylum claim with the home office and they are considered an asylum seeker whilst they are awaiting a decision on that claim. Once the claim is accepted they become a refugee. There is no such thing as an illegal asylum seeker. The UK has signed up to the Universal Declaration of Human Rights (1948), article 14 of the act states that 'everyone has the right to seek and to enjoy in other countries asylum from persecution.'

What is an immigrant?

An immigrant is a person who is entering one country from another to take up new residence. Young people often think that all immigrants are illegal so it is vital to highlight that there is a difference between an immigrant and an illegal immigrant. An illegal immigrant is a person who either enters a country illegally, or who enters legally but subsequently violates the terms of their visa, permanent resident permit or refugee permit.

Who are Gypsies, Roma and Travellers?

Gypsies and Travellers are some of Britain's oldest and longest established ethnic and cultural groups. Gypsies first arrived here more than 500 years ago. That means that they have been a part of British life long before even William Shakespeare or Queen Elizabeth I was born.

There are several different groups of Travellers in Britain, these include:

- Gypsies of England and Wales
- Scottish Gypsies/Travellers
- Irish Travellers
- Occupational Travellers – Showmen/Fairground, Circus
- New Travellers
- Boat People
- Roma

The history of racism
When did racism start?

Forms of racism have been around since the start of history. Prejudice and bad treatment of particular groups of people are widespread in British history and unfortunately, this is probably found in every society of the world today. Ever since people started to travel to different places and meet other groups, there has been conflict as people fought over power, land and money. People often believe that their culture, country and group is better than others' and use this as an excuse to justify treating other people badly.

However, racism in the form that we know it today, where people are divided by the colour of their skin has not always been around. This can be traced back to the transatlantic slave trade where millions of Africans were enslaved by Western countries. At this time there were already some people who believed you could categorise human beings and that some groups were inferior to others. This idea, which of course has no scientific proof, was used by slave owners in an attempt to justify the horrific and inhumane treatment of the enslaved people.

Experiences of racism
What should you do if you hear someone being racist at a football match?

If someone hears racism at a football match, they should take the number of the person's seat and inform a steward or police officer of their behaviour. Racist chanting, or shouting racist abuse, at football grounds is illegal and holds very serious consequences for the perpetrators, such as being

banned from future games or having their season tickets taken away from them. Depending on the severity of the offence and the amount of evidence, there could also be criminal action taken – arrests, fines or even imprisonment.

Dealing with and campaigning against racism
Can racism ever be just 'banter'?

No! Using someone's skin colour or ethnicity as an insult has a deep effect. It implies that it is negative to be of that background, attacks something which is intrinsic to that person and is an attack, not just on the individual, but on other members of their family, community or group too. Allowing 'jokes' or 'banter' about someone's skin colour, religion, nationality or culture creates a society where that behaviour is deemed acceptable and allows for ridicule, name calling, exclusion and stereotyping if left unchallenged.

Are 'Pikey' and 'Gyppo' racist words?

Gyppo and Pikey are extremely racist and offensive towards people from any of the Traveller groups as these terms have a history of being used to hurt and offend. These words should never be used, even if it is towards someone who is not a Gypsy or Traveller.

Is 'black on white' racism dealt with as seriously as 'white on black' racism?

White young people sometimes feel as if nothing would be done if they experienced racism from a person with a different skin colour and that it would be thought of as less serious than if they had been racist to a black or Asian person. It is important to empathise with these young people and to try and understand where these feelings have come from, but it is essential that they realise that racism happens to people of all skin colours and each case, regardless of who is the target and who is the perpetrator, should be treated with equal seriousness. There are no separate laws depending on who has carried out the racism, if any one has reported a racist incident and it wasn't dealt with then they should be encouraged to report it again and insist that something is done.

Is racism illegal?

Yes! In UK law it is illegal for someone to be treated differently or to suffer harassment because they have a different skin colour, nationality or religion (Single Equality Act 2010). It is illegal to commit an offence which incites racial or religious hatred (Racial and Religious Hatred Act 2006) and if someone commits a crime which is racially motivated, it is considered a racially aggravated offence (Crime and Disorder Act 1998) which increases the seriousness of the offence and results in a heavier sentence.

Is it ok to ask questions about why people are different?

Absolutely! We are often fearful to ask people directly about any differences in skin colour, religion, nationality and/or culture they have – we shouldn't be! Not asking people these important questions can lead to people making assumptions about a person, which can then lead to stereotypes and even prejudice towards that person. If you want to know something about a person, for example how they would like you to describe their skin colour or why they are wearing a particular piece of religious clothing, it is best to ask them politely. This is much better than guessing and potentially offending someone!

The Equality Act, making equality real

Information from the Government Equalities Office.

What the Equality Minister says

My name is Harriet Harman. I am the Minister for Women and Equality. Equality is a big part of my job and is very important to the Government.

Equality

This means everyone having the same chances to do what they can. Some people may need extra help to get the same chances.

Equality is right for many reasons.

> ➤ People enjoy life more if they are treated fairly.
> ➤ The country is richer because each and every person can do what they are best at.
> ➤ It is easier for people to live side by side and get on with each other if everyone is treated fairly.

The Equality Act

We needed the Equality Act to make existing equality laws in the UK clearer and stronger and to ensure that all people are treated fairly. The Act became law in 2010, when Parliament agreed it was right.

Stronger laws were needed because the old equality laws did not make equality happen fast enough. For example:

> ➤ Many women are paid less than men for the same kind of work.
> ➤ Clever children from poorer families do less well at school.
> ➤ Disabled people are a lot more likely to have no job.
> ➤ People of different races find it harder to get a job.
> ➤ Many lesbian and gay people are worried about asking the police for help in case they are treated unfairly.
> ➤ Many people who have changed their sex do not use public services like swimming pools because they think they will not be treated well.

The Equality Act brings together nine big equality laws and about 100 smaller laws.

Bringing these laws together makes it a lot easier for employers and other people to know what they must do. It will also help everyone understand the law.

What the Equality Act does

This list shows, in a few words, what the Equality Act does to make the equality laws stronger.

> ➤ The Act tells some public bodies to do two new things to help make equality happen. Public bodies include government departments, schools, hospitals and councils.
> ➤ The Act will mean public bodies have to think about equality when they are buying things.
> ➤ The Act will mean public bodies have to think about equality when they are buying things.
> ➤ The Act has new rules to make sure older people are treated fairly. For example, some shops only help older people if they are with a young person.
> ➤ The Act has two new ideas to make men and women's wages easier to compare.
> ➤ The Act allows employers to use positive action if they want to make sure their workers are diverse.
> ➤ The Act lets employment tribunals do new things to help people get fair treatment. Employment tribunals sort out arguments between employers and workers.
> ➤ The Act protects people who are looking after someone, like carers, from being treated unfairly.
> ➤ The Act makes it clear that women can breast-feed their babies in shops, cafés and other places.
> ➤ The Act makes sure clubs do not treat people unfairly.
> ➤ The Act includes more to stop disabled people being treated unfairly.

These changes and other things in the Act will make Great Britain a better place to live and work, now and in the future.

Two new duties for public bodies

The Equality Act gives public bodies two new duties.

➤ Some public bodies will have to think about how they can help to stop people doing less well than other people because of their family background or where they were born.

➤ All public bodies must think about treating people from different groups fairly and equally.

Using positive action to increase diversity

Positive action

This lets employers and service providers think about equality when looking at who they might supply their services to or employ. It might mean providing services in a different way or giving people information or training. For employers it might mean choosing between two people who can do the job as well as each other.

'The Equality Act and the many other kinds of equality work the Government is doing will make Britain a more fair and equal place for everyone.'

Diverse or diversity

This is a mix of different kinds of people. For example, men and women, young and old people, people of different races, disabled and non-disabled people.

Even when people of different races do well at school and college, they do not get their fair share of the top jobs. For example:

➤ Only 15 Members of Parliament are people of different races. Looking at the diversity of this country, there should be 60.

➤ Only three top judges are people of different races

The Act makes it easier for employers to use positive action and it lets them choose a person who will make their workers more diverse, when choosing between people who are right for the job.

Example

A company needs a new person for one of its top jobs. Currently, all of its other top jobs are done by men. When people apply for the job, the company finds two people are just right for the job – a woman and a man. The company can use positive action to give the job to the woman. This is because it will make the company's top people more diverse. But the company cannot give the job to the woman if the man is better for the job.

Equal pay and equality information

40 years ago a new equal pay law told employers that men and women should get equal pay for doing the same sort of work, but many men still get more wages than women.

To put this right we need to know where it is happening. So the Equality Act includes two new ideas to help make equal pay happen.

➤ If a company has 250 or more workers, it may have to publish information about differences in men and women's pay.

➤ The Act also enables the Government to tell public bodies to publish information about equal pay and how many workers it has who are disabled or people of different races. The Government plans to do this for public bodies with 150 or more workers.

The Act also stops employers telling workers they must not talk to each other about how much they get paid.

Positive action in elections for Parliament and local councils and diversity reporting

An election is when everyone over 18 can vote for the person they want to be their Member of Parliament or their local councillor.

It is important that the people in Parliament and on local councils are as diverse as the people in the country. That is not happening yet. It is already possible for political parties to choose only women for elections in some areas. The Act will let political parties have these women-only lists until 2030.

The Equality Act also lets political groups help some people like people of different races and lesbian, gay and bisexual people have a chance to get elected. The Act also lets the Government make political parties publish information on the diversity of their candidates.

Extra powers for employment tribunals

Employment tribunals can suggest how an employer can put things right for a worker if they were treated unfairly. But most of the time this does not help the employer's other workers, because most people who complain to employment tribunals have stopped working for the employer.

The Equality Act allows the employment tribunal to tell the employer their advice, and that it should apply to all of their workers, even when the one who complained doesn't work there any more.

Example

A man of a different race complains because he says his employer has treated him unfairly because he is a of a different race. The employment tribunal agrees, but the man has stopped working for the employer. The employment tribunal can tell the employer how to change the way they do things so their other workers of different race are treated fairly in future.

Making Britain fair and equal for all

The Equality Act helps many of the different groups of people in England, Scotland and Wales who sometimes get treated unfairly.

The Equality Act and the many other kinds of equality work the Government is doing will make Britain a more fair and equal place for everyone.

Information is from the Government Equalities Office and is reprinted with permission from GOV.UK. © Crown Copyright 2013

www.gov.uk

Mini glossary

Public bodies – *an organisation whose work is part of the work of the Government, but which is not a Government department.*

Diversity – *A mix of different kinds of people. For example, men and women, young people and older people, people of different races, disabled and non-disabled people.*

Employment tribunal – *public bodies that resolve disputes between employers and employees.*

Equal Pay Act – *introduced in 1970, this Act states that men and women who are equally skilled and doing the same work should be paid equally.*

Are the people in Britain ethnically diverse?

'We celebrate the diversity in our country, get strength from the cultures and the races that go to make up Britain today.' Prime Minister Tony Blair, 2 October 2001

People from all cultures and ethnicities can be found in every corner of Britain and each person in his or her own way has contributed to make Britain the place it is today.

If you walk down a street in Britain, especially in the bigger cities you will usually see people with different hair, skin and eye colours. They may have white, brown or black skin and blonde, brown, black, or red hair, with blue, black, brown or green eyes. Many of the people you see will be British people but they all look different because the people of Britain are a diverse race. Not all British people are Christian and/or white.

How Britain became a mixed race society

Britain is, and always has been, a mixed race society. Early in our history we were invaded by Romans, Saxons, Vikings and Norman armies and later Africans were brought to Britain by force in the seventeenth and eighteenth centuries as slaves or servants. Over

the years, thousands of people have arrived in Britain as refugees from France, Ireland, Russia and other countries, escaping from persecution or famine in their own countries.

There are British people whose parents first came to Britain in the 1950s and 1960s from the Caribbean, India, Pakistan, Hong Kong and other places. Their homes are mainly in the big English cities like London, Birmingham and Manchester.

About 8% of the population of Britain today are people from other cultures and ethnicities. That is 4.6 million people.

According to a BBC Report in September 2005, immigration made up more than half of Britain's population growth from 1991 to 2001.

250 different languages are spoken in London every day.

The Guardian newspaper reported in 2007 that the latest government estimate for long-term net immigration to the UK is 145,000 a year.

New Cultures

People moving to Britain have brought their own cultures and try to keep two cultures alive. An excellent example of this is the Notting Hill Carnival which celebrates Caribbean Culture and is now a very big part of British life today.

People from minority ethnic groups are more likely to live in England than in the rest of the United Kingdom. They made up nine per cent of the population of England in 2001 compared with two per cent of the population of both Wales and Scotland and one per cent of the population of Northern Ireland. Nearly half (45 per cent) of the total minority ethnic population live in London.

Timeline: immigration to Britain

1100s
Merchants come from Netherlands and settle.

1500s
Queen Mary marries Philip of Spain.
Dutch and French Protestants settle.

1600s
Asians brought to England as Slaves.

1700s
Refugees from the French revolution (1789) arrive. First records of Chinese sailors in London.

1800s
Jewish arrivals fleeing persecution in Poland, Ukraine and Belarus.
Irish settlers escaping poverty during the famine in Ireland.
Trade brings Indian and Chinese people to main ports.
Jews flee to UK from Russia and Poland.

1900s
1914 – More than 250,000 Belgian refugees fled to the UK, escaping the fighting of the First World War.
1930s – Refugees from Nazi oppression arrive in the UK.

1940-1960 – Polish people homeless because of the War, invited to come to UK.

1948 – The boat Windrush brings 492 Jamaicans to the UK – thousands more follow. Immigration from Caribbean encouraged to help rebuild post-war Britain.

1950s and 60s – Settlers from other new Commonwealth nations arrive – India, Pakistan and Bangladesh.

1970s – East African, Asians and Vietnamese arrive.
1972 – Asians expelled from Uganda; 27000 admitted to UK.

1980s – African community expands. Refugees arrive from Eastern Europe – Romania and former Yugoslavia.

1991 – Break up of the Government of Somalia lead to 7,500 applications being made to the UK many of which are accepted.

1992-1997 – 2,500 Bosnians enter the UK as refugees following the break up of former Yugoslavia.

1999 – Renewed heavy fighting in Sri Lanka leads to 5,130 applications for asylum being made to the UK.

The above information is reprinted with kind permission from Project Britain.
© Mandy Barrow 2011

www.projectbritain.com

All together now?

A portrait of race in Britain.

Two Britons, born in the same year as Stephen Lawrence, describe their experiences of race relations in this country.

Radha Jenkins, Mother

Radha Jenkins' parents were both British. Her mother was mixed race, her father is white. She lives in north London with her three children, Taylor, Liam and Lene

Some people used to have a go at my mum because they couldn't understand how this black woman had two white children. And even now when I fill in those forms there's not really a box for me – sometimes I tick 'white' and sometimes I tick 'other', but I do wonder why we have to be put in a box. Why can't we just stand outside it? In family pictures it's like 'spot the white person', because most of my family are a shade of brown. It bothered me that I was different when I was little, but my mum would tell me I was her English rose.

I've mainly been out with white guys, but my sister, who's olive-skinned, only really goes out with black guys. But I'm not really a black guy's idea of a good girlfriend. There's this cultural thing of a lot of black men wanting their women to be dressed up, have their hair and nails done and the rest – I can't be bothered with that. When I was about 18 I went out with an Irish guy and I remember when his mum found out that mine was mixed race she said to me, 'Oh, you could get away with being Irish, couldn't you?' That shocked me, what did she mean 'Get away with it'?' – as if having a mixed race mum was something you should hide.

I sometimes think there's more racism today – particularly with kids. There's more segregation and people are more anxious. You used to have three distinct groups: there were white people, Asian people and black people and they mostly sort of stuck in their specific groups. Now that people are so much more mixed it seems like everyone's racist against everyone. It used to be gangs of black kids versus gangs of white kids, but now it's much more complicated. When I was younger everyone just hung around with each other, but now there's Somalian gangs, for example, who maybe don't like the Polish and the Polish kids don't like the black kids, or whatever. When did this happen?

When Stephen Lawrence was killed everyone thought it was horrific, now almost every day you hear about some kid that's been knifed or shot. My eldest son's 13 and I worry about him all the time. I even called the police once because he was late home. He sometimes has this big, blonde afro and I remember once I was walking behind him down the street and two older black guys walked past him and said: 'Check out the white boy with his afro!' I wondered if maybe he gets that all the time. It looks amazing and unique, but some people don't like difference.

On 22 April 1993, a black teenager named Stephen Lawrence was murdered in a racist attack. The case has been described as 'one of the highest-profile racially-motivated murders'. The trials and events this case triggered helped to change the UK and many things in British life, such as laws and reforms to public services. In January 2012, Gary Dobson and David Norris were finally found guilty of Lawrence's murder.

Abdul Chohan, Assistant head teacher
Abdul Chohan teaches at a school in Lancashire. His parents are both Indian

I'm the assistant head of a school in Bolton where there are 40 languages spoken. Here, there's tolerance – it's built in as so many different cultures are part of the playground, so the staff have got to recognise that and take into account the different needs of kids from different faiths and cultures. It wasn't like that even five years ago, when I started. Then it was just white British and Indian and Pakistani. When I was at school, it was a different world. There was such a big divide between the two groups of children: the white British kids and then the Indian and Pakistani kids. Now, the kids in my school are so much more integrated – for example, I've got this Sikh boy from Afghanistan, the first Sikh at our school. When he came I had a chat with him and he said he was a bit scared, but now he's fitted into a group made up of one lad from Afghanistan, a lad from Senegal and a Kurdish boy, so there's this foursome of friends who really get on, even though they're all completely different and speak different languages.

When tensions arise it's usually to do with geography, and you get turf wars between different groups. So, for example, the Pakistani kids are located in one area and the Indian kids in another area, and when they fight people assume it's racial, although it's actually just because they're from different parts of town. I was speaking to a colleague of mine from Liverpool and she was saying it's the same with Catholics and Protestants. So sometimes I think: is it a race thing or is it just boys being boys? If I look at the same lads when they're much older, the 30-plus generation in Bolton, there's no tension there; it's gone by then.

I don't think my ethnicity – the fact that my parents are from India – has much of an influence on anything. When I go to India it's very alien to me. Years back I went to Pakistan and Nepal, but after two months all I could think of was a cheese-andonion pasty and I wanted to be back in Bolton. The weather's not great here, but this is home.

I think the challenges now are more to do with religion than race. Especially after 9/11 and the 7/7 bombings. It's strange how someone who's been brought up here practising their religion can suddenly feel quite alienated. Islam was a big part of my upbringing, and because of that I feel like I'm trying to be an ambassador for my religion all the time, trying to promote myself and who I am. But what I say to the boys I work with is that in a lot of countries if you want to practise your faith you're in handcuffs, but you have your freedom to practise your faith over here, the freedom to do so many things. That's one of the main reasons I'm proud to be British.

www.equalityhumanrights.com/raceinbritain

Challenging discrimination

Tackling hate and harassment.

The links between hate crime, discrimination and prejudice

Hate crimes are part of a larger scale of discrimination, and discrimination is founded in prejudice.

The 'Pyramid of Hate' shows the steps between behaviour that we might encounter on an everyday basis, up to extreme acts of violence. If we don't challenge the less severe acts of prejudice at the base of the pyramid, this can lead to an environment in which hatred and discrimination grow.

Challenging discrimination

Challenging discrimination and prejudice are key to preventing hate crime. It is always important to challenge discriminatory behaviour, but it can be difficult, especially if you fear the response of the person you challenge. You should only directly challenge discrimination if you feel it is safe to do so. If you do not feel safe, report the behaviour using your organisation/school's policies and procedures. The following guidelines can help you to challenge in an effective way.

A challenge should be an invitation, not an attack

Very few people think of themselves as prejudiced. People are unlikely to respond positively to an accusation that they are. They may respond by defending their attitude instead of questioning and changing it. For example, if a stereotype was made against a particular ethnic group, ask them where their view came from? How many people from that group do they know?

Challenge the behaviour, not the person

Invite the person to question their own behaviour and attitudes, so that you can understand what they are saying and reassess their language and attitudes. Avoid labelling them. Focus on what they have said or done, rather than who they are.

Educate them by providing facts if you have them

For example, a common prejudiced view is that asylum seekers come to England and have everything handed to them on a plate. An appropriate challenge to this would be 'Did you know most asylum seekers want to work but the law prevents them from doing so?'

Stay calm

If you say something calmly, showing consideration for the other person's feelings you are more likely to get through to them than if you shout or become aggressive. Try to say something like 'When you say that it makes me feel…', 'What you are saying could be offensive. What makes you think that I am not gay/disabled/ etc.?' By admitting to your own feelings you are also acknowledging theirs.

Talk about 'I' not 'You'

For example 'I find your jokes offensive and not very funny', instead of 'You are racist.'

Be heard

Don't expect the other person to agree with you. Just make sure they have heard what you have said.

Have a private word

Go back to people afterwards if you can't think of the most effective way to challenge them at the time.

Ask for support

Ask for other people's support either in helping you decide how to challenge the behaviour, or in joining the challenge.

Mini glossary

Hate crime – a violent crime that is motivated by prejudice towards someone's race, ethnic origin, sexual orientation etc.

Genocide – purposely killing, on mass, people from a particular nation, religion or ethnic group.

Prejudice – forming ideas and opinions about someone without getting to know and experience them first.

Scapegoating – pinning the blame on someone else for problems and/or wrongdoings (this person becomes a 'scapegoat').

The above information is reprinted with kind permission from Chesterfield Law Centre. © Chesterfield Law Centre 2013

www.chesterfieldlawcentre.org.uk

Pyramid of Hate

Genocide
The deliberate, systematic extermination of a race/group of people

Violence
Against people   Against property

Threats   Arson
Assault   Desecration
Terrorism
Murder

Discrimination
Employment-based   Personal harassment
Housing-based   Education-based

Acts of prejudice
Name calling   Social avoidance
Telling belittling jokes   Ridicule   Social exclusion

Prejudiced attitudes
Accepting stereotypes   Scapegoating
Not challenging stereotypes/prejudices

Activities

Brainstorm

1. What is racism?

2. What do people mean when they say that Britain is 'ethnically diverse'?

Oral activities

3. In small groups, discuss whether you think white people can be the victims of racism. Make some notes on your discussion and feedback to the rest of your class.

4. With a partner, take it in turns to role play a situation in which one of you is being discriminated against because of your race. This discrimination could take place in the workplace, the classroom or in a social situation. Discuss how you felt when you were playing the part of the person who was being discriminated against.

Moral dilemma

5. One of your friends tells a racist joke that you feel is inappropriate but they dismiss it as 'banter'. How would you deal with this situation? What could you say to your friend?

Research activities

6. Research the murder of Stephen Lawrence. Write a short essay summarising the case and discussing why it was so important.

7. Create a questionnaire to find out about racist bullying in your school. You could ask people about their ethnic origin, whether they have experienced racist bullying and what form that bullying took. Write a summary of your findings and include some graphs or tables to demonstrate your results.

Written activities

8. Imagine that you are the parent of a child who is being bullied because of their race. Write a letter to your child's school explaining the situation and suggesting steps that you think the school should take in order to help.

Design activities

9. Create a poster that will raise awareness of racism in schools.

10. Create a PowerPoint presentation that explores your background and heritage.

Racism in the classroom

Racism is the unfair treatment, or hatred, of individuals of a certain race. Racism may be practised to benefit one race, or simply because one or more other races are thought to be inferior. Unfortunately, racism may still exist in classrooms across the United Kingdom.

Racism and the law

The Race Relations Act 1976 protects individuals from being discriminated against on the grounds of colour, race, nationality, religious beliefs or ethnicity. This Act does not distinguish between whether racist practices were deliberate or not, it is concerned only with the fact that racial discrimination occurred. This Act covers discrimination faced in employment, education and more.

Racism and education

Racism can be experienced in four main ways:

➤ Direct discrimination: Is deliberate and obvious.
➤ Indirect discrimination: Occurs when practices or policies disadvantage one or more racial groups.
➤ Harassment: Occurs when an environment is allowed to become hostile for members of a certain race.
➤ Victimisation: Occurs when someone has complained about racism and is then treated less fairly than others.
➤ These actions are all in breach of the Race Relations Act 1976.

Racist bullying by other pupils

Racist bullying by other pupils can take many forms, from hurtful comments to physical attacks. In order to stop such bullying, students should first familiarise themselves with their school's anti-bullying policy. Then students should record instances of bullying in a diary, including what happened and who was involved, and tell a trusted adult about the incidents. Any proof of bullying, such as defaced property or hurtful electronic communications, should be saved. Online abuse, whether via text messages, emails, instant messages, websites or blogs, should also be saved. When ready, the student and his or her parents should confront the school and make a formal complaint according to the school's procedures and policies.

> **Pause for thought...**
>
> ➤ What is your school's anti-bullying policy? Do you know what steps you should take if you need to complain about an incident of bullying? Ask a teacher and find out.

Racist bullying by teachers

Unfortunately, bullying by teachers, towards pupils, may occur in school. Teachers may make degrading comments about a student, engage in unwanted or hostile physical contact with a student, make unwanted or suggestive sexual contact with a student, say inappropriate or lewd things to or about a student, or even suggest to a student that his or her grade depends on something other than his or her studies. If a student feels that they are being subjected to racist bullying or discrimination by a teacher, the student should ask for a meeting with both the teacher and the department head. Parents may want to be at this meeting as well. If it is believed that nothing has come from the meeting then a formal complaint should be filed with the school. In the meantime, the student should discuss transfer options as a way of being removed from that teacher's class. It may not be fair that the student has to leave, but safety should be the first priority.

Racism is disgusting in all forms but, unfortunately, it does still exist. Individuals who encounter racism in the classroom should be prepared to document and report this type of bullying. If the educational institution itself does not respond to these complaints then it might be wise to seek professional, legal advice about the situation.

15 September 2012

www.aboutequalopportunities.co.uk

Eight-year-olds are suspended for race abuse in Derbyshire schools

Children as young as eight are being excluded from Derbyshire schools for racially abusing fellow pupils and staff, shock statistics have revealed.

Incidents have included one pupil telling a Polish student to go back to his own country and another of a 10-year-old verbally abusing a sports coach.

Freedom of Information requests made by the Derby Telegraph have revealed there have been at least 42 fixed-term exclusions for racial abuse at schools in Derbyshire in 2012.

These included at least five children aged eight or nine.

In the past five years there have been a total of 387 exclusions for racial abuse across the county with the numbers staying similar from year to year.

Kirit Mistry, executive director of Derby Racial Equality Council, said he believed the figures were 'just the tip of the iceberg' as many incidents go unreported.

He said there had also been incidents which he had heard of but which he believed schools had not done enough about.

Mr Mistry said: 'Head teachers meet on a regular basis. Racial abuse should be on their agenda for discussion.

'They should see statistics for this regularly. That way there is some confidence that this is being dealt with.

'But the key is that parents need to report incidents. They need to write a formal letter to schools' boards of governors.'

He said that, in particular, tension between Eastern European nationalities and other groups had been on the rise, due to increased immigration from those countries.

Mr Mistry said: 'Some children pick up racist ideas from their parents but some get it from their peers, which is why schools need to deal with it.'

But schools insist they are taking a tough-line with racist behaviour.

And Lynda Poole, director of learning and inclusion at Derby City Council, said the authority would expect its

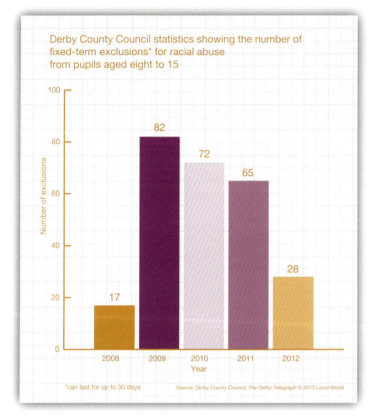

Derby County Council statistics showing the number of fixed-term exclusions* for racial abuse from pupils aged eight to 15

*can last for up to 30 days   Source: Derby County Council, The Derby Telegraph © 2013 Local World

schools to 'cover the topic of racial abuse as part of their social development curriculum'.

Phil Dover, head teacher at Lees Brook Community School, which has excluded three pupils so far this year, said it had strong anti-racism policies.

He said: 'In two cases, the exclusion was for racist name-calling and the third was a case of a student telling another (Polish) student to go back to his own country.

'Incidents such as these are always treated seriously and fixed-term exclusions were given because the students involved ignored very clear warnings that had been given in assemblies to the whole school.'

Mr Dover said his staff had recently noticed an increase in the number of incidents of 'racist name-calling and the use of racially-insensitive language' at the school.

He said: 'Being strongly anti-racist is particularly important in a school like Lees Brook where, historically, there has been a very small number of students from minority ethnic backgrounds.

'This has risen steadily in recent years from 1% to 7% against a national figure of 22%.

'There are now an increasing number of students from Eastern European countries.'

He added that the school had been praised in its recent Ofsted inspection for the work it does towards community cohesion.

Linda Sullivan, head teacher at Dale Primary School, said a 10-year-old had been given a two-day fixed-term exclusion this year for racially abusing a member of staff – the first the school handed out in six years.

Mrs Sullivan said: 'It was abuse against a member of our sports team who was working after school.

'It was unacceptable behaviour, unacceptable terms were used.'

Statistics show that, in 2012 so far, there have been 14 fixed-term exclusions of pupils aged eight to 15 from 12 Derby schools for racial abuse.

In 2011 there were 29 fixed-term exclusions; in 2010, 18; 2009, 30; and 2008, 32.

Derbyshire County Council statistics show that, in 2012, there have been 28 fixed-term exclusions for racial abuse, of pupils from age eight to 15. In 2011 the figure was 65; in 2010, 72; 2009, 82; and 2008, 17.

Fixed-term exclusions can last for up to 30 days but are more commonly five or less.

Mrs Poole said that all schools were required to have a racial abuse policy, adding that Senior School Improvement Officers work with schools to ensure that polices are operational.

A county council spokeswoman said the authority worked closely with schools to 'eliminate racial abuse'.

She said: 'Examples of the support provided by the council include the 'Holding Together' publication which provides schools with curriculum plans, model policies and access to further information sources from within the council and beyond.'

The Department for Education defines 'racial abuse' as, racist taunting and harassment, derogatory racist statements, swearing attributed to racism, racist bullying, or racist graffiti.

12 June 2012

www.thisderbyshire.co.uk

What if they'd said 'Jew'?

Today, most people in the U.K would be shocked and appalled if they encountered acts of anti-Semitism (racism towards Jewish people) – perhaps because of its connection to the Second World War. When Braveheart actor Mel Gibson allegedly directed an anti-Semitic rant towards a Jewish policeman, the world's media was outraged, his fans were angry and many people claimed he would never work in Hollywood again. If his comments had been made about a Traveller, Gypsy or Roma person, would they have caused such a scandal? Probably not. And this is precisely what the Traveller Solidarity Network is trying to highlight.

The 'Network believes that racism towards Travellers, Gypsies and Roma people is the last remaining, socially acceptable, form of racial discrimination in the UK and, to emphasise its prevalence, they have created a thought-provoking website: Jewify.org.

From the home page of Jewify.org, users can copy and paste the url of any news article or website about Gypsies, Travellers and Roma people – and see how they feel when it is turned against Jewish people instead. The user's chosen article is opened up in a new window, and looks just like the original – except the words 'Gypsy', 'Traveller' or 'Roma' are replaced with the word 'Jew'.

The Traveller Solidarity Network hopes that Jewify.org will raise awareness of racism against Gypsies and Travellers, and highlight the need for change.

5 February 2013

Pause for thought...

➤ Try this yourself: find an article or website about Gypsies, Travellers or Roma people and replace these words with 'Jew'. How do you feel when you read this new version?

'We intend to make a census to see who lives in Jew camps, who has a right to stay and to live in humane conditions'

'Italy starts controversial plan to fingerprint Jews'

'Anger at Jewish invasion'

'Sarkozy orders all Jews expelled from France'

'Bill for evicting 90 Jewish families from the UK's biggest illegal site'

The above article was written by Cara Acred, on behalf of Independence Educational Publishers. © Cara Acred/Independence Educational Publishers Ltd.

Police racism: 293 cases, five dismissals

As the CPS recommends a Met Police officer is charged for racially abusing a suspect during last year's riots, Channel 4 News can exclusively reveal the number of cases of racism among UK police.

The incidents range from racist language in emails to the use of the n*** word.**

The figures, obtained under the Freedom of Information Act, date back to the Macpherson report 13 years ago which followed the death of black teenager Stephen Lawrence and led to the Met Police being labelled 'institutionally racist'.

Also on Tuesday, a review by the Crown Prosecution Service (CPS) found 'sufficient evidence' to charge Met Police officer Alex McFarlane with a 'racially aggravated public order offence', and has now advised the Independent Police Complaints Commission (IPCC) to press charges.

The officer was accused of using racist language against a 21-year-old black man, and was apparently recorded by the suspect on his mobile phone.

In April 2012, Channel 4 News revealed 120 race cases inside the Met and just one dismissal during the same time frame. This data, gathered from 31 forces in England, Scotland, Wales and Northern Ireland, completes the national picture.

Channel 4 News can reveal that between 1999 and 2012:

- ➢ 293 police officers were disciplined for racist behaviour
- ➢ 749 were referred to the IPCC
- ➢ Five were dismissed
- ➢ Seven were forced to resign.

Of all the 749 cases referred to the IPCC, 513 were within the Metropolitan Police.

One of the officers who was dismissed in 1999, used insulting and abusive language to another police officer, saying: 'Michael, that's why we keep down n******.' The officer was disciplined by being forced to resign, but on appeal, was dismissed.

Another officer from the same police force was reported in 2006, for interrupting a briefing about treating members of the community equally. He stood up and said: 'B*******! They're all black b******* and I hate them all.' The case was not referred to the IPCC and the PC was given a warning.

In many of the cases, officers were fined or given a written warning for inappropriate racist behaviour. One was fined for sending an email including 'inappropriate and racist terminology' from the police server.

Prosecution 'is necessary'

In a statement following her review of PC McFarlane's case, Alison Saunders, Chief Crown Prosecutor said: 'I have taken the decision in this case that, as well as there being sufficient evidence...a prosecution is necessary in order to maintain confidence in the criminal justice system.

'It is regrettable that the original decision was wrong, but I hope the action taken and my decision today demonstrates the willingness of the CPS to review its decisions independently and swiftly and to take appropriate action where necessary.'

The decision comes as Scotland Yard confirmed last week that ten cases are being referred to the Independent Police Complaints Commission (IPCC) after fresh allegations of racist comments earlier this year.

17 April 2012

www.channel4.com

Confronting indirect racism

Information from About Equal Opportunities.

By Beth Morrisey

> **Racism can take many forms. Direct racism occurs when something obvious and blatant is said or done. Indirect racism occurs when something subtle occurs. The 'hidden nature' of indirect racism makes it very hard to identify, and even harder to challenge. Types of indirect racism include:**
>
> - ➢ benign ignorance
> - ➢ jokes and banter
> - ➢ imitations
> - ➢ Mockery.
>
> These kinds of behaviour should be challenged, just as long as you remain safe while doing so.

Confronting indirect racism

Refusal to engage

Refusal to engage may involve:

- ➢ staring,
- ➢ making comments about someone of a difference race (but not speaking directly to them),
- ➢ remaining silent around someone of a different race,
- ➢ looking past or through someone or a different race, or ignoring them.

These actions are often designed to make the individual feel like an outsider. You could challenge this behaviour by introducing yourself and forcing a conversation, or even drawing attention to the unacceptable behaviour. If these tactics don't help, then ignoring the behaviour and joining another group for small talk might be an easier way to get through an event.

Benign ignorance

'Benign ignorance' occurs when someone thinks they are acting in a helpful or complimentary way when, actually, they are causing offence. Often, a person thinks they are being nice and doesn't understand that their behaviour is actually hurtful or degrading, or based on stereotypes and prejudice. When you are faced with an example of benign ignorance, don't be afraid to let the other person

know why their assumptions make you uncomfortable. You could say something like 'Thank you, but I think my abilities are due to my studies and talents rather than my race'. This is a polite way to confront the issue, keeping the conversation as polite as possible at the same time.

Jokes and banter

Jokes and banter can be hard to challenge because the people involved tend to say things like 'But I was just joking!' or 'It was just a bit of fun!'. Use this excuse to let them know why you didn't find something funny, or why it wasn't fun for you to have to listen to their thoughtless words. This tactic works best if you were not joining in the jokes and banter at any point. If nothing else, try to get everyone involved to agree to avoid racist jokes and banter in the future even if you can't get them to understand why you haven't found their previous words and behaviours all that amusing.

Imitations and mockery

Like jokes and banter, imitations and mockery are often defended as just a bit of fun – even when someone points out that imitating an accent or mannerism might be hurtful. These excuses can be deflected by letting people know that even if they didn't mean anything by it, whether they think you are too sensitive or not, you were still hurt.

15 September 2012

Pause for thought...
- ➢ **Can you think of any examples of benign ignorance? Have people ever made assumptions about you because of your appearance or race?**

www.aboutequalopportunities.co.uk

Online racism

Law targets racism on social networking sites.

By Nick Branch

A number of recent cases have highlighted the disturbing amount of racism on social networking sites such as Twitter, prompting celebrities and footballers to quit the site and sparking a debate on how racism can be tackled online.

Recent cases include a student who was jailed after posting a racist comment about the collapsed Bolton midfielder, Fabrice Muamba. Another similar case involved a student at Newcastle University. Joshua Cryer, 21, admitted using the social networking site to post racist abuse about the former Liverpool striker, Stan Collymore.

The Crown Prosecution Service is using a variety of laws to bring these foul-mouthed bigots to justice. Joshua Cryer was charged under section 127 of the Communications Act, for sending grossly offensive messages, including racist taunts, to Collymore. He was sentenced to a two-year community order, 240 hours community service and ordered to pay £150 costs.

The case concerning Fabrice Muamba was perhaps even more striking given the condition of the Bolton midfielder and the public outpouring of support for him and his family. Liam Stacey, a 21-year-old Biology student at Swansea University was charged with making racially aggravated comments about him as he lay fighting for his life. He is due for sentencing this week, and has been warned that he could face a custodial sentence for his remarks.

Prosecutors are keen to ensure that events which take place online are treated with the same force as those which occur in public. Legal action is easier to pursue as online accounts can be traced, and evidence is automatically held on servers. Faced with this, offenders usually plead guilty, avoiding any significant police involvement with the case.

Wendy Williams, head of the Crown Prosecution Service in the north-east, said:

'In recent months we have seen a number of similar cases in the north-east, in which people have been racially abused through social networking sites. Ironically, the strongest evidence in each of these cases has been directly provided by the defendants themselves.'

'When a person makes such comments digitally, they effectively hand police and prosecutors much of the evidence needed to build a robust case against them,' she added.

28 March 2012

The above information is reprinted with kind permission from FindLawUK.
© FindLawUK 2012

blogs.findlaw.co.uk

Jail for student in Muamba Twitter race rant a perversion of justice

Information from Index on Censorship.

Swansea student Liam Stacey has been sentenced to 56 days for a 'racially aggravated public order offence' after tweeting a very poor taste joke about footballer Fabrice Muamba followed by several racist and inflammatory comments.

No wonder it's called Twitter. Only twits use it!

The 21-year-old claimed he had been drinking all day and was quite drunk by the time he'd sent tweets. This is most likely true. It was St Patrick's Day and the last day of the Six Nations rugby championship, and quite a lot of people would have spent that day in the pub. But while it may be true, it's hardly a defence.

Is Stacey a racist? A troll? A drunk and mouthy young man? Possibly a little of each. But none of these are illegal. Stacey's conviction is for a public order offence.

One can understand why public order laws exist. The police may need to be able to take people off the streets to prevent imminent violence, and be able to punish people for causing disruptions.

But was there actually any risk that Stacey was threatening public order? I don't think there was. A row on Twitter is not the same thing as shouting abuse in the street, where there may be immediate physical consequences. Twitter may be like a pub, in the sense that it's a space for social interaction, but it's definitely not the pub in that when tempers fray, no one's going to get glassed. The worst that will happen is someone will block you.

Only one of Stacey's tweets was violent in nature, and that did not contain any racial abuse. So has he been jailed for eight weeks solely for being offensive at a time when people on Twitter were congratulating themselves for the outpouring of goodwill to the fallen Muamba? If so, then people who care about free expression should be very, very worried.

27 March 2012

blog.indexoncensorship.org

Mini glossary

Troll – *Internet slang for someone who intentionally posts a comment or remark online that will provoke a reaction. These remarks are often hurtful or inflammatory.*

Racism in football

Information from The Culture, Media and Sport Committee.

Racism in football has become significantly less common in the UK due, in part, to changes in wider society but also because of awareness campaigns and codes of conduct put in place by the sport's governing bodies and the Professional Footballers Association. The Football Association, Premier League and Football League have, for example, developed codes of conduct for staff, players and fans as well as funding and promoting anti-racism campaigns by organisations such as Kick it Out and Show Racism the Red Card.

Recent incidents of racist abuse in the UK, both on and off the pitch, have highlighted the fact that racism is a continuing problem. Some of the evidence we have heard, as well as recent media coverage, have demonstrated that social media has become both a tool for the spread of racist and abusive content and a potential means of combating the ignorance and prejudice that lie behind such behaviour. We believe that the football authorities should be using this developing forum for communication and debate, to spread positive messages about equality and diversity and also to speak out against instances of racist abuse when they occur.

The atmosphere experienced by those attending football matches has changed hugely since the 1970s and 80s when racial and other forms of abuse were common. Match attendance has become much more of a family-friendly activity and clubs continue to introduce measures to try to improve the standards of behaviour at matches. However, there remain significant problems ranging from homophobic abuse to what is often described as 'laddish behaviour' on the terraces. Transparent and consistent methods for reporting criminal behaviour including racism are still lacking, in particular at grass roots level. There is also a clear need to encourage more candidates from ethnic minorities to train as coaches and referees to ensure that clubs and boards can select from a more diverse pool of recruits from within the football pyramid.

While the general level of progress in combating racism and racist abuse is positive and should be applauded, there is much more that can and should be done.

19 September 2012

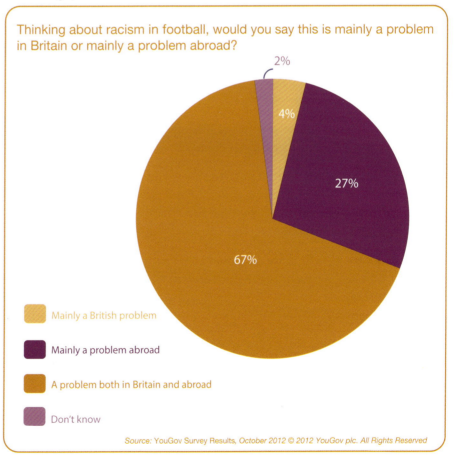

Thinking about racism in football, would you say this is mainly a problem in Britain or mainly a problem abroad?

- 2%
- 4%
- 27%
- 67%

Mainly a British problem

Mainly a problem abroad

A problem both in Britain and abroad

Don't know

Information from the Culture, Media and Sport Committee and is reprinted with kind permission from the House of Commons. © Crown Copyright 2012

www.publications.parliament.uk

Record number of 'racist' attacks on English in Scotland

Anti-English rhetoric is at risk of 'creeping' into Scottish society after police reported a record number of racist attacks against white Britons, it has been claimed.

By Simon Johnson, Scottish political editor

Police recorded 1,295 racist incidents in 2011/12 where the victim was white and British. The total is up a quarter on the previous year and 57 per cent more than in 2004/05.

The category includes both attacks on English people and incidents where the victim is Scottish and the perpetrator is from an ethnic minority.

But the vast majority of perpetrators were also white, suggesting that many cases involved racism against the English.

SNP ministers said they were 'very disappointed' by the figures but opposition parties said racist attacks against English people should be treated with the same seriousness as those directed at ethnic minorities.

The overall number of racist attacks increased by ten per cent last year, with the largest number of incidents directed against the Pakistani community.

However, while the number of Pakistani victims has fallen markedly in recent years, attacks against white Britons have increased and they are on course to become the ethnic group most likely to be subjected to racism.

Willie Rennie, the Scottish Liberal Democrat, leader said: 'We cannot allow anti-English rhetoric to creep into society and the SNP government must to all it can to combat this.

'While racism against some ethnic groups is falling, it is still far too prevalent in Scottish society. This includes racist abuse directed towards the English, which is just as bad as any other form of racism and cannot be tolerated.'

John Lamont, Scottish Tory chief whip, added: 'If it is an increase in anti-English behaviour from those living in Scotland, we have to treat it with the same severity we do any other racist incident.'

But Christopher Thorpe, a doctor in cultural sociology at Aberdeen's Robert Gordon University, said he thought the police were recording more cases because people were becoming less tolerant of racist attitudes.

The Scottish Government figures showed there were 5,389 racist attacks last year, an average of 15 per day and the first increase in five years. The record total compares to 4,911 in the previous year.

Broken down by the ethnic origin of the victims, they showed that 23 per cent of attacks (1,357) were directed against Pakistanis and 22 per cent (1,295) against white Britons.

Since 2004/05, the number of incidents with Pakistani victims has fallen from 1,773, a drop of nearly a quarter.

Over the same period the total involving white Britons has increased from only 826 and is on course to become the most common type of racist attack. More than four out of five perpetrators last year (83 per cent) were also white and British.

Only three per cent of wrongdoers were Asian, suggesting the vast majority of attacks were white-on-white and English people were the victims.

Men aged between 26 and 35 were the most likely victims, while perpetrators were most commonly men aged 20 or younger.

Roseanna Cunningham, the Community Safety Minister, said: 'Scotland has an outstanding reputation as a welcoming and tolerant nation and we cannot let a minority of people tarnish our image.

'Regardless of the reasons for the increase, we must continue with the work we are doing to tackle racism and hatred in all its forms whilst constantly looking at new ways of getting across the message to the next generation of young Scots.'

12 December 2012

www.telegraph.co.uk

White people paid more and ethnic pay gap widening

Researchers from the University of Essex found that in 1993 white people earned an average of 18p an hour more than non-whites, but by 2008 the gap had risen to 43p an hour. This was around 7.5% of the minimum wage for those over 21 in 2008, or 3.6% of median hourly earnings.

The research by Dr Malcolm Brynin at ISER and Dr Ayse Güveli, from the Department of Sociology at the University of Essex found that Britian's white workers are paid more than ethnic minorities and the hourly pay gap has more than doubled in the 15 years to 2008.

The research published in the latest edition of the journal Work, employment and society, Dr Brynin and Dr Güvel analysed more than 650,000 results from UK's large-scale quarterly Labour Force Survey.

They say that most of the gap between whites and non-whites was caused because non-whites found it harder to get into well-paid professions and trades.

The analysis shows not only that the ethnic pay gap varies considerably by ethnic minority but that it is in large measure the result of occupational segregation.

However, even where the two groups worked in the same profession or trade, there was a gap in pay – by 2008 whites were earning an average of 43p an hour more than non-whites doing the same type of work. This compared to 1993 when whites earned an average of 18p an hour more than non-whites in the same profession or trade.

They found that the overall gap had widened despite the fact that the proportion of people in most ethnic minorities groups working in managerial jobs was about the same as whites by 2008 – around 45%. This was probably because non-whites tended to be in lower levels in the job hierarchy.

'In Britain white people earn more than people from ethnic minorities on average. However, this gap is generally less when the pay of white people is compared to that of ethnic minorities within occupations. The wage gap therefore derives in significant measure from occupational segregation. Where a negative pay gap occurs it is because ethnic minorities tend to cluster into low-paying occupations.'

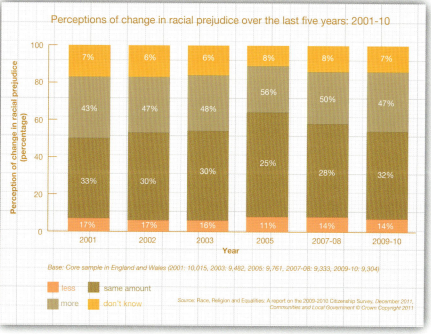

Perceptions of change in racial prejudice over the last five years: 2001-10

Base: Core sample in England and Wales (2001: 10,015, 2003: 9,482, 2005: 9,761, 2007-08: 9,333, 2009-10: 9,304)

less   same amount
more   don't know

Source: Race, Religion and Equalities: A report on the 2009-2010 Citizenship Survey, December 2011, Communities and Local Government © Crown Copyright 2011

'This sorting is due in part to personal factors such as education but some is almost undoubtedly because minorities find it harder to enter better paid occupations.'

'When we try to understand the determinants of wages controlling for a range of factors, it is clear that on this basis most ethnic minorities earn consistently less than white people, if not always by much. One implication is that some minorities do not earn as much as their education would warrant.'

28 August 2012

⬦ The above information is reprinted with kind permission from the Institute for Social & Economic Research.
© 2012 Institute for Social & Economic Research

www.iser.essex.ac.uk

Mini glossary

Occupational segregation – *the distribution of people in a job based upon demographic characteristics, such as gender or ethnicity.*

One in three Brits admit they are racist

One in three Brits admits they are racist. A third admitted regularly making comments or being involved in discussions which could be considered racist and more than one in ten admitted they had been accused of being a racist by someone close to them. Furthermore, almost 40 per cent confessed to using the phrase 'I'm not a racist, but …' when discussing race issues facing Britain today.

These worrying figures emerged through a OnePoll survey of 2,000 adults who were asked to honestly express their feelings about foreign nationals living and working in this country.

Alarmingly, many felt their animosity towards foreigners was passed down by previous generations. But the country's immigration policy also emerged as a trigger for emotions which could be considered racist.

The true extent of the racist undercurrent within the country was revealed in this nationally representative study in which 88 per cent of the respondents classed them-selves as 'White British'.

What constitutes being racist will always be a contentious issue, with what one person deems inappropriate the next person may not. Likewise, life experience and cultures we have grown-up in are inevitably going to influence our beliefs and the language we use.

The study also found one in five accept the fact that people around them make disparaging remarks about different ethnic groups – and are not bothered by it.

Age-wise, the over 55s were found to have the biggest chips on their shoulders, with the 18-24 age range close behind. The younger of these two brackets were also more likely to admit making racist comments or partaking in behaviour which could be deemed racist.

The Government's immigration policy was slammed by many of those who took part in the study. Seventy one per cent said they felt the 'open doors' approach to foreign nationals was leading to an increase in racist feelings. As many as one in six demanded Britain close its doors to anyone who is not a UK national.

It's alarming that so many people are just accepting the racist behaviour around them. The findings did show that immigration policy was fuelling the fire for racist behaviour amongst some adults. However, immigration and race are two separate issues although these findings show that many believe one is a consequence of another.

30 May 2012

The above information is reprinted with kind permission from OnePoll.
© OnePoll 2012

www.news.onepoll.com

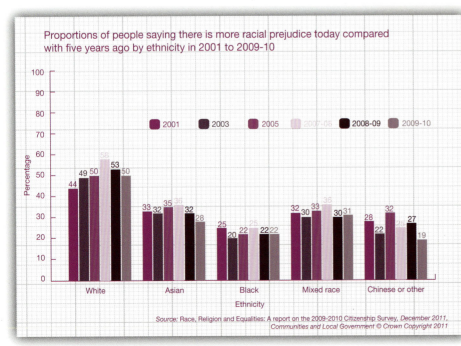

Proportions of people saying there is more racial prejudice today compared with five years ago by ethnicity in 2001 to 2009-10

Source: Race, Religion and Equalities: A report on the 2009-2010 Citizenship Survey, *December 2011,* Communities and Local Government © Crown Copyright 2011

Activities

Brainstorm

1. What is the Race Relations Act 1976?

2. What does the term 'indirect racism' mean?

Oral activities

3. As a class, debate the following statement: 'Social networking sites, such as Twitter and Facebook, encourage people to be racially abusive'.

Moral dilemma

4. Some people wish to remove racially offensive terms, like 'n*****', from books that were published a long time ago. For example, *The Adventures of Huckleberry Finn* (published in England in 1884). With a partner, discuss whether you think this is a necessary change, or a form of censorship.

Research activities

5. Visit the Kick it Out! website (www.kickitout.org) and research their *Let's Kick Racism Out of Football* campaign. Write some notes about what else could be done to tackle the issue of racism in football.

Written activities

6. Watch one of the following films and write a review exploring its portrayal of racism in America: you can choose either *The Colour Purple* (1985), which is set in the 1930s, or *The Help* (2011), which is set in the 1960s. To take this further, find a classmate who chose a different film from you and discuss what you learned about racism in America in the 1930s and 1960s.

Design activities

7. Choose one of the articles from this book and draw your own illustration to accompany that article.

8. Imagine that you are working for an anti-racism charity. Think of a name for your charity and design a product, featuring your charity's logo, that you could sell for £1.99 to raise money. For example, a wrist band, badge, pen or mug.

Key facts

▶ *The Equality Act 2010 makes it illegal to discriminate on the grounds of race, including in employment and in the provision of goods and services. (page 1)*

▶ *In 2011/12 there were 5,389 racist incidents, compared with 4,911 in 2010/11. (page 1)*

▶ *In 2011/12, 44% of victims of racist attacks were of Asian race - i.e. Indian, Pakistani, Bangladeshi, Chinese, or other Asian. (page 1)*

▶ *Only 15 Members of Parliament are people of different races. (page 6)*

▶ *Only three top judges are people of different races. (page 6)*

▶ *250 different languages are spoken in London every day. (page 8)*

▶ *On 22 April 1993, a black teenager named Stephen Lawrence was murdered in a racist attack. The case has been described as 'one of the highest-profile racially-motivated murders'. The trials and events this case triggered helped to change the UK and many things in British life, such as laws and reforms to public services. (page 11)*

▶ *The Race Relations Act 1976 protects individuals from being discriminated against on the grounds of colour, race, nationality, religious beliefs or ethnicity. (page 15)*

▶ *Between 1999 and 2012: 293 police officers were disciplined for racist behaviour, 749 were referred to the IPCC, five were dismissed and seven were forced to resign. (page 19)*

▶ *Swansea student Liam Stacey has been sentenced to 56 days for a 'racially aggravated public order offence' after tweeting a very poor taste joke about footballer Fabrice Muamba followed by several racist and inflammatory comments. (page 22)*

▶ *4% of respondents to a recent survey said that racism in football is mainly a British problem, 27% said it is mainly a problem abroad, 67% said it is a problem in both Britain and abroad and 2% don't know. (page 23)*

▶ *Police recorded 1,295 racist incidents in 2011/12 where the victim was white and British. (page 24)*

▶ *Researchers from the University of Essex found that in 1993 white people earned an average of 18p an hour more than non-whites, but by 2008 the gap had risen to 43p an hour. This was around 7.5% of the minimum wage for those over 21 in 2008, or 3.6% of median hourly earnings. (page 25)*

▶ *One in three Brits admits they are racist. (page 26)*

Glossary

Discrimination – *Unfair treatment of someone because of the group/class they belong to.*

Ethnic minority – *A group of people who are different in their ancestry, culture and traditions from the majority of the population.*

Gypsies and travellers – *Gypsies and travellers have traditionally pursued a nomadic lifestyle which involves moving around from place to place. English gypsies and Irish travellers are protected under the Race Relations Act. This is because they are members of a community with a shared history stretching back over hundreds of years and are recognised by the law as a distinct ethnic minority group.*

Harassment – *A behaviour that is usually persistent and is intended to cause distress and offence.*

Racism – *The belief that one race is superior to another/behaving in a negative or harmful way to someone because of their race.*

Racial discrimination – *Racial discrimination occurs when a person is not treated as well because of their colour, race, nationality or ethnic or national origins.*

Racial prejudice – *Feeling hatred towards another race just because they are different (thinking that their race is better in comparison).*

Reverse discrimination – *When trying to address social inequalities, sometimes reverse discrimination occurs. This occurs when discrimination is directed towards the dominant group in society in order to favour the usually disadvantaged minority group. People sometimes refer to this as 'positive discrimination'.*

Multiculturalism – *A number of different cultures living, and interacting, side-by-side, for example within a school or a country.*

The Race Relations Act 1976 – *The Race Relations Act 1976 aims to promote race equality and good race relations. It does this by making it against the law to discriminate against anyone because of their race (this refers to someone's actions rather than their opinions and beliefs). It is not necessary to prove that the other person intended to discriminate against you: you only have to show that you received less favourable treatment as a result of what they did.*